HOLLY SNOW

The Little Girl Who Wanted to Make Toys

by

Fred Cornetta

Illustrated by Tim Privette

Icicle Publishing

10 MT. VERNON ST. #116 • WINCHESTER, MA 01890

To my daughter Sarah – Fred C.
To my son Matthew – Tim P.

Text copyright © 1998 Fred Cornetta
Illustrations copyright © 1998 Tim Privette

Book design, typography, and production by
Arrow Graphics, Inc., Watertown, MA
Printed in Hong Kong

ISBN: 0-9658318-2-5
LC: 97-93560

Many years ago Holly Snow was adopted by Santa and Mrs. Claus.

As Holly grew, her favorite place was the toy shop. She watched the elves hammer and saw, carve and paint.

They made special toys for Holly, and would hide them for her to find. Holly climbed over benches, crawled under tables, and looked everywhere until she found one of the special treasures. Her nose crinkled and her eyes sparkled when she found a brightly colored toy or stuffed animal.

H er best friend was Shoo, the family cat.

One day when she was older Holly said to everyone, "I want to make toys. Just like you! Please let me try?"

The elves gathered around. They were puzzled. No one except elves had ever made toys before. "She is just a little girl," they thought. "She is not a toymaker."

Holly pleaded with the elves, but they wouldn't listen.

Through the corner of her eye – she spotted some paint.

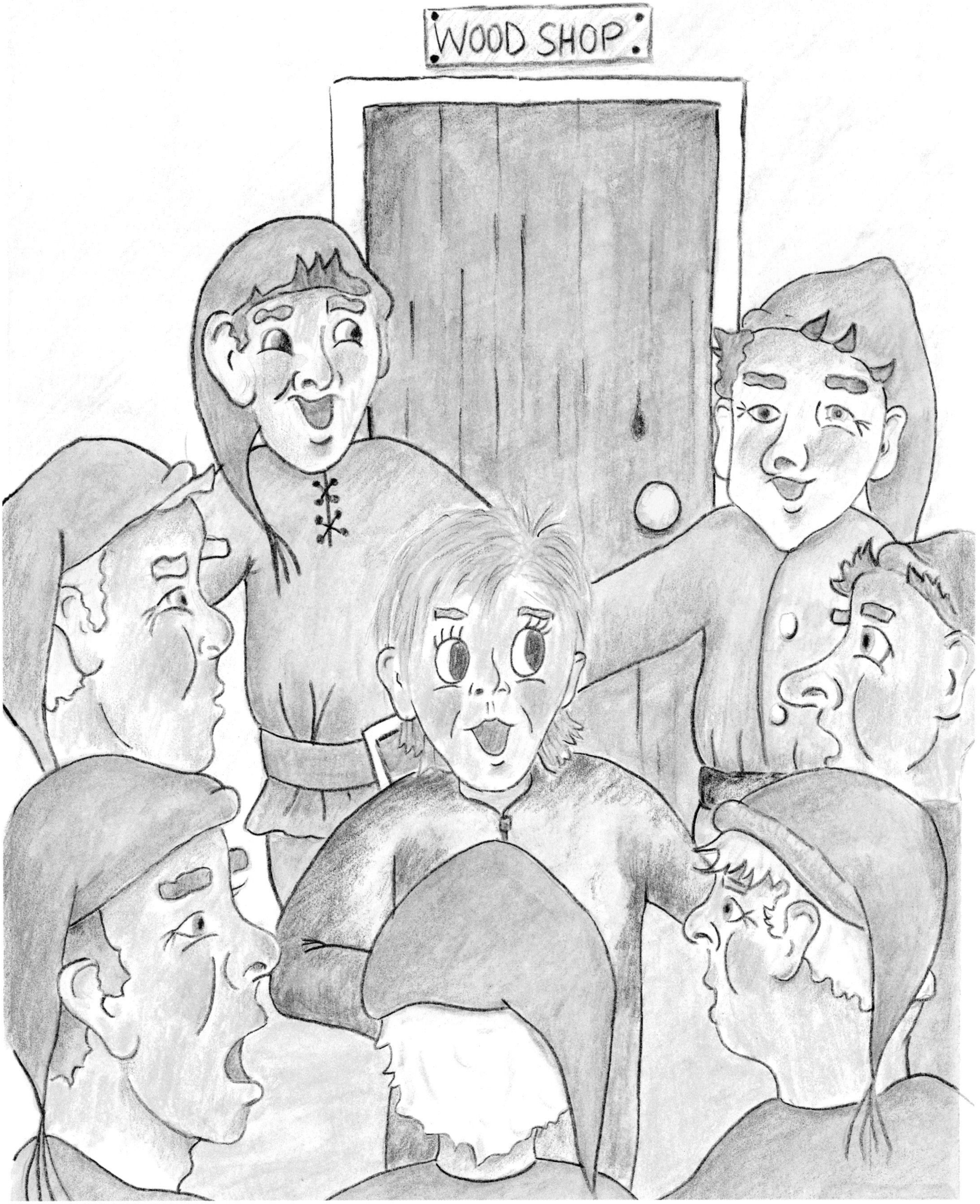
WOOD SHOP

Holly smiled and sang as she painted.
"HO! HO! HO! Golly gee! I make toys. LOOK AT ME!"

"STOP!" shouted the oldest and wisest elf. "This isn't right. You're not an elf. Only elves can make toys. It's always been done that way."

"But I want to help," said Holly. "I know I can do it."

The old elf just turned away. "Everyone get back to work. We have to finish before dark, before the ice people come out."

Holly hung her head in sadness. The elves did not listen. No one gave her a chance. She left the toy shop … alone.

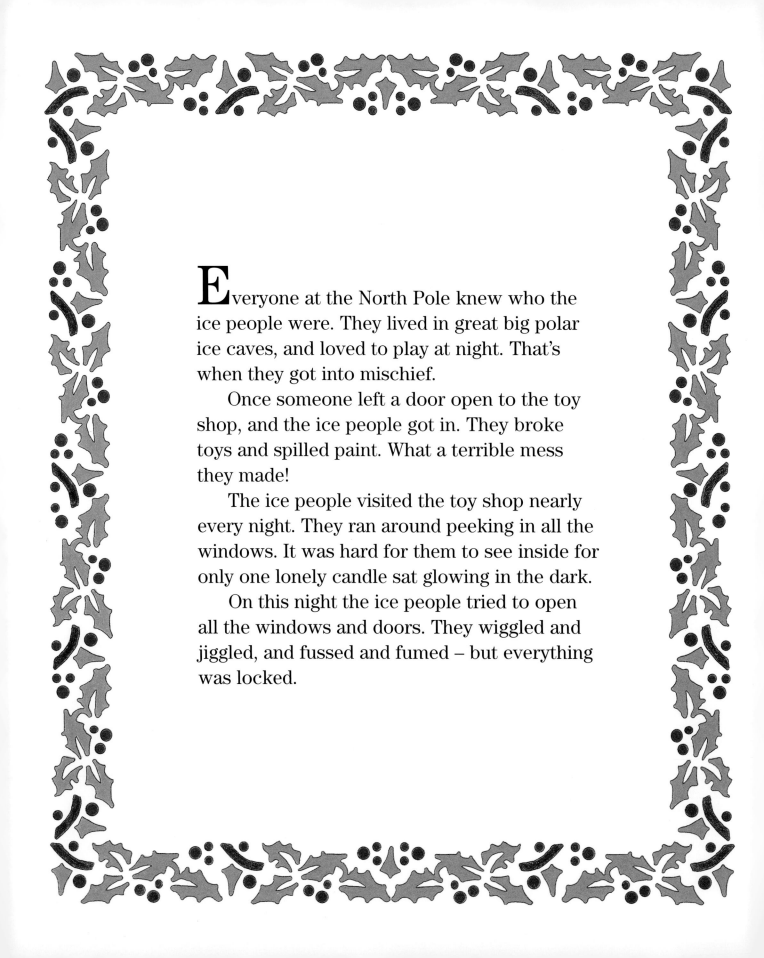

Everyone at the North Pole knew who the ice people were. They lived in great big polar ice caves, and loved to play at night. That's when they got into mischief.

Once someone left a door open to the toy shop, and the ice people got in. They broke toys and spilled paint. What a terrible mess they made!

The ice people visited the toy shop nearly every night. They ran around peeking in all the windows. It was hard for them to see inside for only one lonely candle sat glowing in the dark.

On this night the ice people tried to open all the windows and doors. They wiggled and jiggled, and fussed and fumed – but everything was locked.

"I know I can make toys … if only the elves would give me a chance," Holly said.

"Well, Holly," said Santa, "maybe now is not the right time."

"But when will be the right time?" asked Holly.

"Perhaps when you're a little older …"

Holly started to sniffle. She was very sad.

Santa gave her a gentle hug. "Don't worry, Holly, it will be all right."

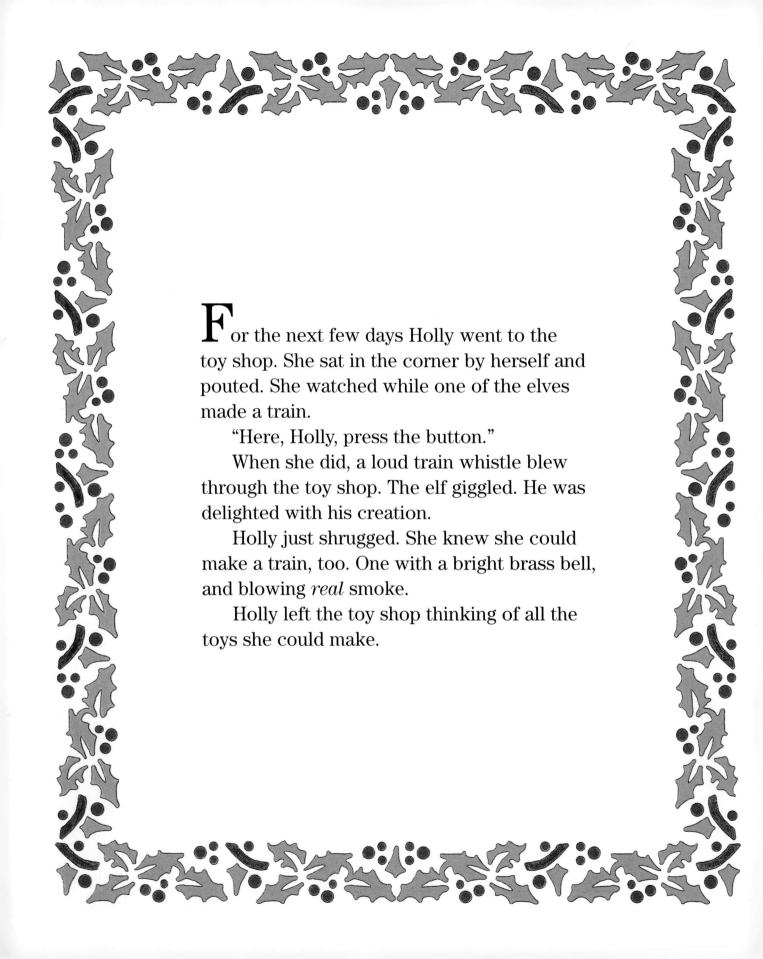

For the next few days Holly went to the toy shop. She sat in the corner by herself and pouted. She watched while one of the elves made a train.

"Here, Holly, press the button."

When she did, a loud train whistle blew through the toy shop. The elf giggled. He was delighted with his creation.

Holly just shrugged. She knew she could make a train, too. One with a bright brass bell, and blowing *real* smoke.

Holly left the toy shop thinking of all the toys she could make.

"Oh, Shoo how can I show them that I can make toys, too?"
Shoo sat quietly looking up.
"It's not fair," she said. "If only they would let me, there would be more toys for everyone – even for you."
Shoo purred and licked her lips.
Holly stared into space. "Hmm, I wonder."

It wasn't easy sneaking into the room where the elves hung their coats without making a noise. The elves were asleep in the next room. Holly tiptoed. She had to be careful not to make a sound. She did not want to wake the elves. Then she spotted the keys to the toy shop.

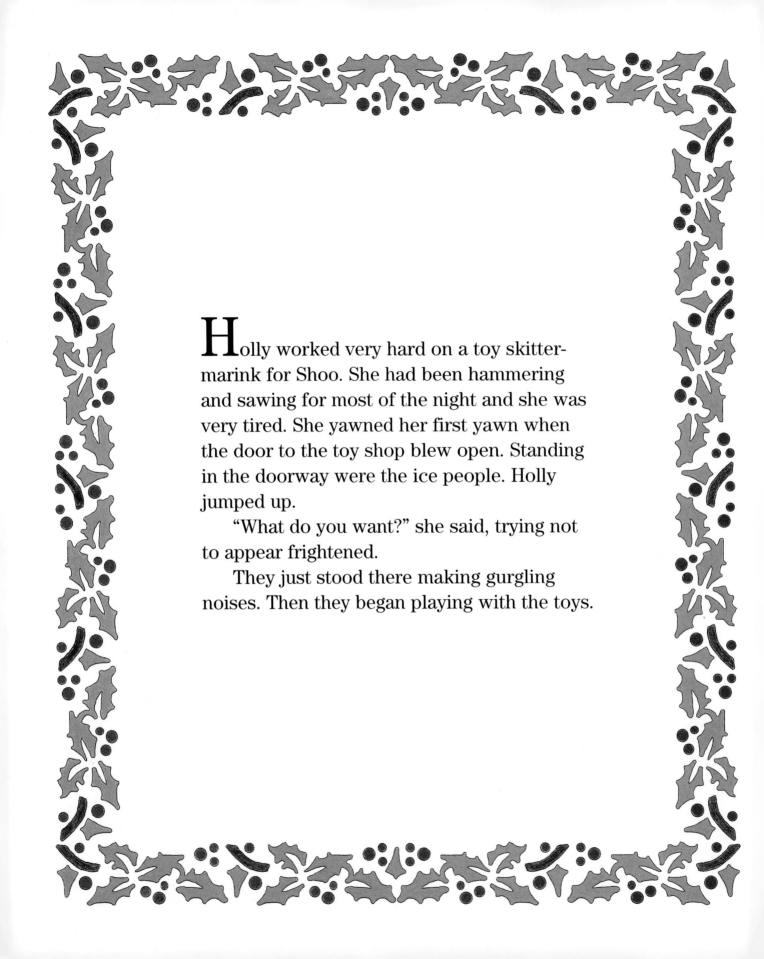

Holly worked very hard on a toy skitter-marink for Shoo. She had been hammering and sawing for most of the night and she was very tired. She yawned her first yawn when the door to the toy shop blew open. Standing in the doorway were the ice people. Holly jumped up.

"What do you want?" she said, trying not to appear frightened.

They just stood there making gurgling noises. Then they began playing with the toys.

"NO!!!" shouted Holly. But the ice people kept playing.

No matter what Holly said or did, the ice people kept playing. They crashed and bumped into everything. Toys smashed against the floor. Decorations shattered into a million pieces.

Finally, the ice people stopped. It was getting too warm in the toy shop for them.

Sunlight peeped through the window. The ice people had to leave.

"Go home all of you!" Holly shouted. "Go home or … or … or you'll melt."

The ice people were scared. Afraid of melting they ran home to their ice caves as fast as they could.

Holly looked around the room. "This place is a wreck!"

She grabbed a broom and started to sweep. It was no use. There was not enough time to clean everything up. The elves were sure to blame Holly. "I'll never get the chance to make toys now," cried Holly.

When the elves arrived at the toy shop they stared at the mess.

They couldn't believe their eyes.

"I'm sorry," said Holly. I was making a skitter-marink for Shoo when the ice people got in. They did it! I couldn't stop them."

"But you knew you were not supposed to be in here," said the oldest and wisest elf.

Holly knew she had disappointed them very much, but the elves said nothing more. They knew they had to get to work to make sure there would be enough toys for Santa to deliver on Christmas Eve.

"I must do something, Shoo," said Holly as she put the finishing touches on a little toy. Shoo sat listening. "This is all my fault. We can't leave out anyone this Christmas. It wouldn't be fair."

She thought and thought. And after a long time she said, "I've got it! I can make toys. Right here in my room. No one will know."

One by one, Holly was able to sneak tools from the toy shop. She secretly made toys … all sorts of toys.

There were cars, boats, and trains. Dolls, balls, and planes.

She stuffed them in the closet. She hid them under the bed. Holly's room became her own little toy shop.

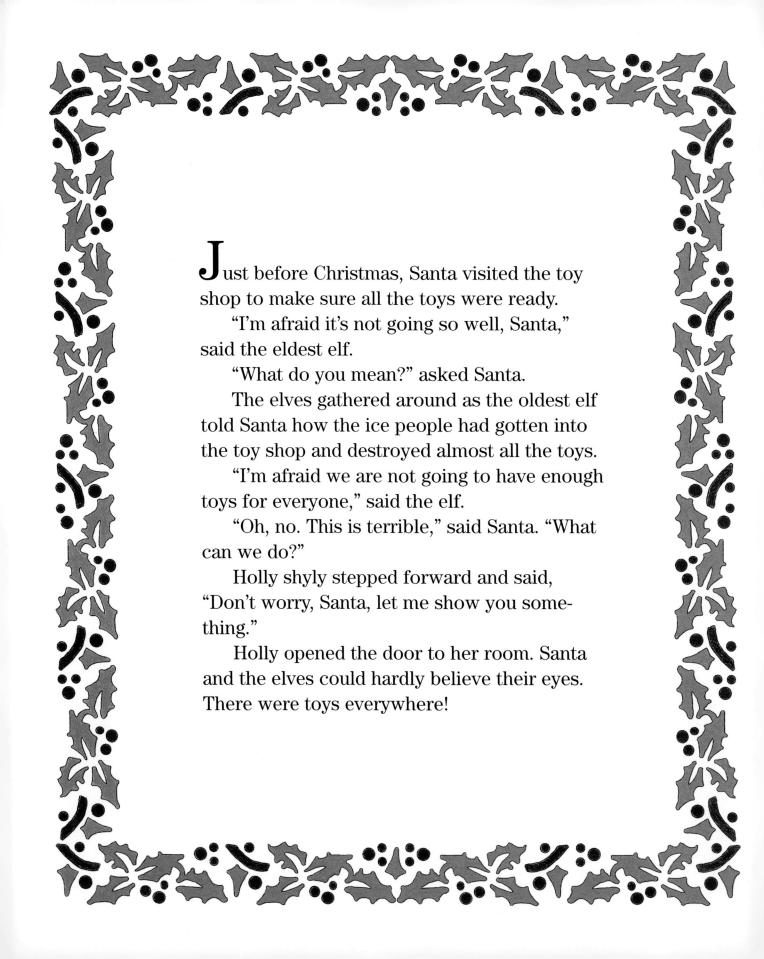

Just before Christmas, Santa visited the toy shop to make sure all the toys were ready.

"I'm afraid it's not going so well, Santa," said the eldest elf.

"What do you mean?" asked Santa.

The elves gathered around as the oldest elf told Santa how the ice people had gotten into the toy shop and destroyed almost all the toys.

"I'm afraid we are not going to have enough toys for everyone," said the elf.

"Oh, no. This is terrible," said Santa. "What can we do?"

Holly shyly stepped forward and said, "Don't worry, Santa, let me show you something."

Holly opened the door to her room. Santa and the elves could hardly believe their eyes. There were toys everywhere!

Santa Claus packed the sleigh and said good-bye to everyone on Christmas Eve. He gave Holly Snow a great big hug and kiss before mounting his sleigh.

"Thank you, Holly," Santa said. "You really are a toymaker."

Holly smiled and wished Santa good luck. She felt so proud of herself as she watched Santa take off into the night to deliver toys and good cheer to everyone all around the world.